Written by Rick Warren

Words To Love By

Illustrated by Ag Jatkowska

ZONDERkidz

For my favorite people in the whole world . . .
Kaylie, Cassidy, Caleb, Cole and Claire..

–RW

For Eddie with all my love.

–AJ

LORD, may these words of my mouth please you.
And may these thoughts of my heart please you also.
You are my Rock and my Redeemer.

PSALM 19:14 (NIrV)

ZONDERKIDZ

Words to Love By
Copyright © 2018 by Rick Warren
Illustrations © 2018 by Ag Jatkowska

Requests for information should be addressed to:
Zonderkidz, 3900 *Sparks Drive, Grand Rapids, Michigan* 49546

978-0-310-75282-0

Design: Kris Nelson/StoryLook Design

Printed in China

18 19 20 21 22 /DSC / 21 20 19 18 17 16 15 14 13 12 11 10 9 8 7 6 5 4 3 2 1

Did you know

you have the power to change someone's life with your words?

I love you.

Words may be small, but they can do

BIG
Things

Bright
delightfu
Jolly A
you're valuable   believe   F

Words can **encourage.**

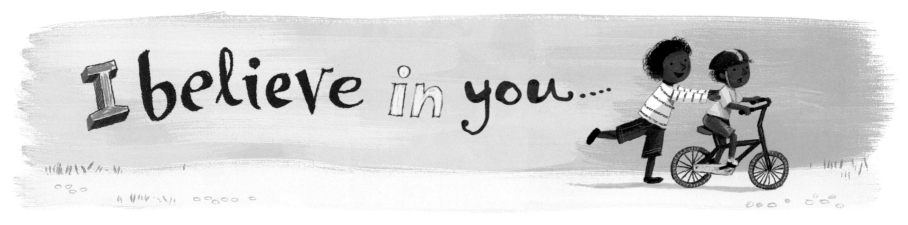

I believe in you...

...you're going to be great.

...you're really good at that.

They can bring out the best in people.

...I knew **you** could do it!

...well done! you did it!!

This *is* beautiful!

Words can spread **Love** and **Kindness**

Do you need help?

Let me HELP you...

Thank you...

Please share...

and let others know **they're not alone.**

Do you want to play with US?

Words can show **respect**...

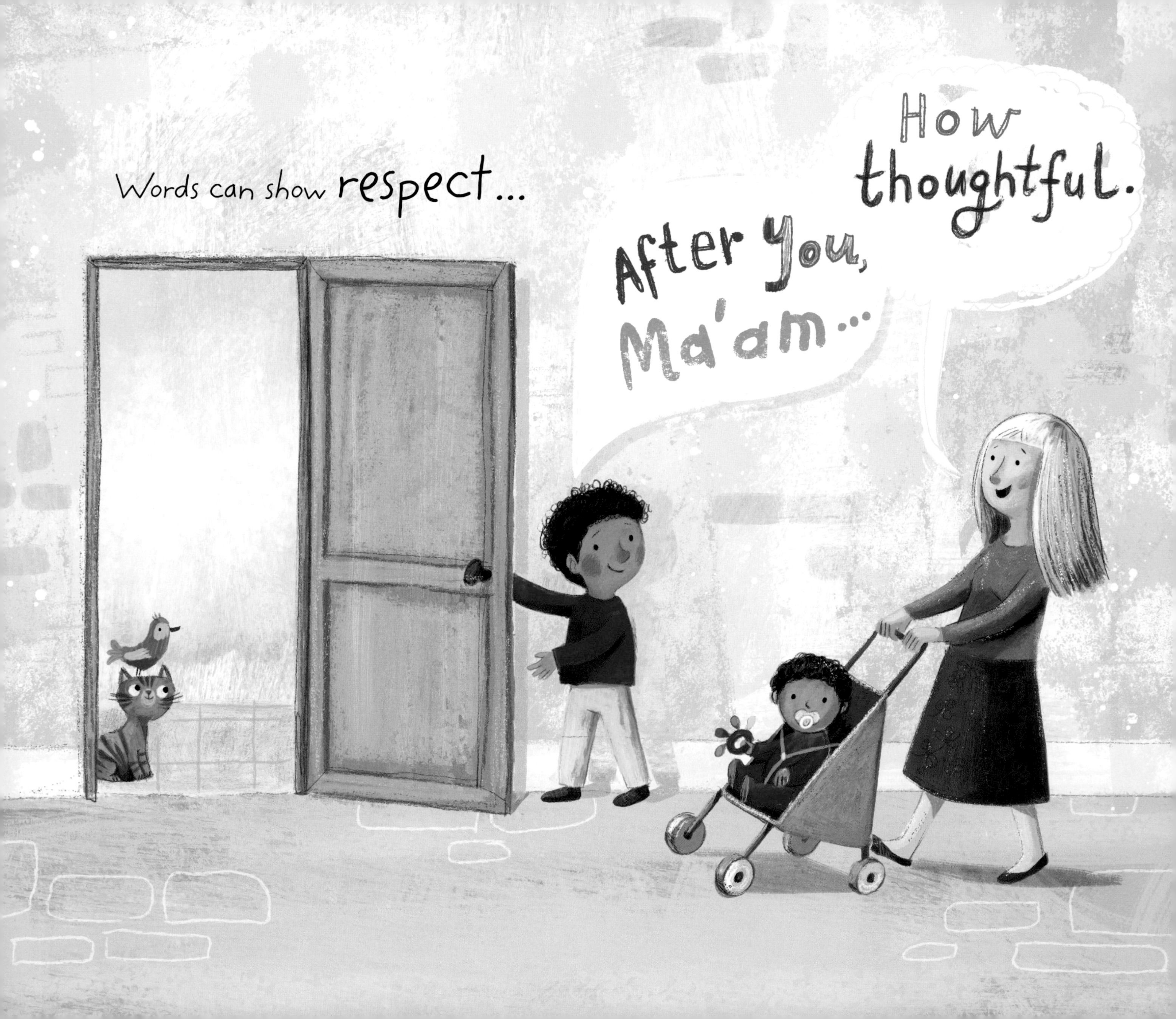

and let the world know how **thankful** we are.

Thank you from the bottom of

my heart!

That makes me smile.

Words can **heal**...

I'm Sorry.

I forgive you ...

and help build friendships.

Sometimes words are spoken in **anger**.
And unkind things are said that you don't really mean.

So, **be careful** with your words. Once you send them out into the world, you can't get them back.

Why don't you leave me alone

I don't like you!

The words you use show others **what's in your heart.**

God wants you to have a heart filled with **kindness and love.**

Words are powerful and should be used wisely.
They can steer you in the direction you want to go.

kind

SMILE Like

forgive

Love

Do you

want to share

appreciate

Nice

If you don't like where you're headed, try changing the way you talk.

I'm happy for you

I care

Love

I'm grateful. please

Sometimes it's best not to speak at all.
Sometimes it's better to just LISTEN.

But always keep in mind...
The words you choose today can **change your life**...

And someone else's too.